The
Runaway
Whale

Written by Keith Faulkner
Illustrated by Jonathan Lambert

Longmeadow Press

The little whale had always longed
To see the world unknown.

And so one day as mother dozed
He slipped away alone.

He swam in search of coral seas
Across the ocean blue.

To go exploring on his own,
It was his dream come true.

"I'm off to see the wide, wide world,"
He told a friendly stranger.

He was too young to understand
The world is full of danger.

He didn't think about his mother
Searching for her son.

He didn't think of anything
Apart from having fun.

Throughout the sunlit oceans
He played the whole day through

And there was no one else around
To tell him what to do.

He traveled far beneath the waves,
Guided by the sun's bright light.

But then he felt alone and scared
When daylight slowly turned to night.

Next day a strange sound overhead
He'd never heard before

Chased him through the sea for miles
'Til he could swim no more.

The little whale soon realized
He missed his mother so.

But when he thought that he'd go home,
Which way was he to go?

He searched the seas from shore to shore,
He swam each coast and bay,

And very soon began to wish
He'd never run away.

At last he heard his mother's call —
A welcome, joyful sound!